KU-226-204

Let's Play!

Deborah Niland

This is Red Dog.
Is he diving?

No!
He is hanging from the
monkey bars.

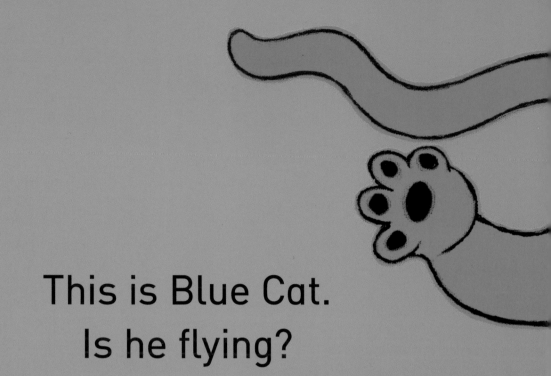

This is Blue Cat.
Is he flying?

No!
He is jumping on
the trampoline.

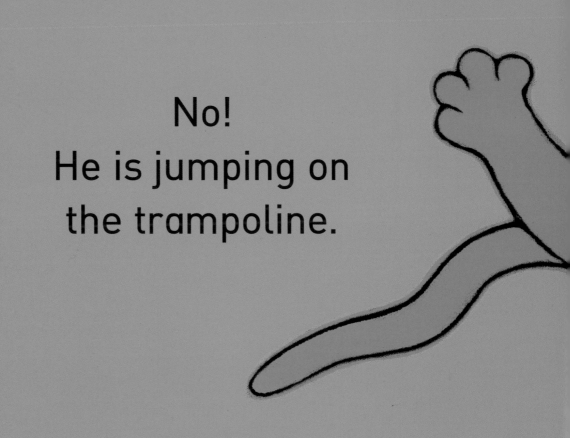

This is Yellow Bird.
Is she sleeping?

No!
She is whizzing
down the slide.

Red Dog gets off the swing.
It's making him dizzy.

He pushes Blue Cat
and Yellow Bird
on the swing instead.

'Higher!' says Blue Cat.
'Higher!' says Yellow Bird.

Blue Cat makes a big sand castle.
He sits on top.

'I'm the King of the Castle,'
sings Blue Cat.

'Can I be King of the Castle too?'
asks Red Dog.
'Yes,' says Blue Cat.

'Can I be Queen of the Castle?'
asks Yellow Bird.
'Yes,' says Blue Cat.

Oh no!
They all fall down.

'What fun!' says Yellow Bird.
'Let's do it again!'